baxter™
goes to
Imagination Land

AUTHOR & ILLUSTRATOR
Jenn Duggan

Follow my adventures at
baxterthedogbooks.com

THANK YOU
To my family and friends
(furry and not)
for being a constant source
of love, support and inspiration.

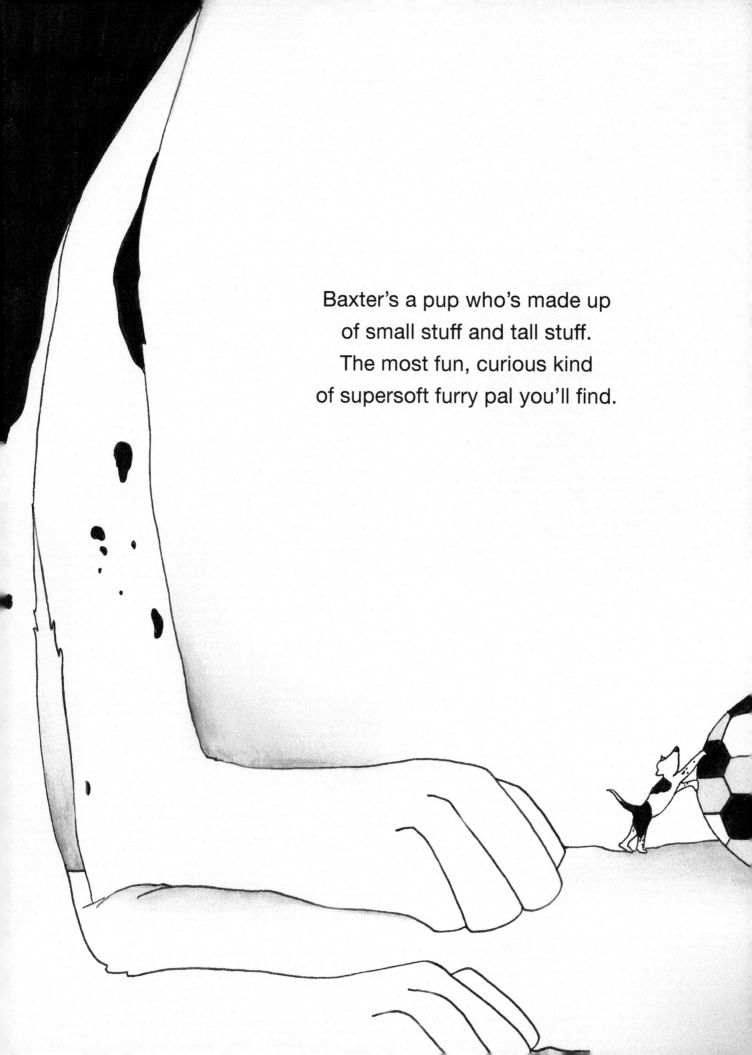

Baxter's a pup who's made up
of small stuff and tall stuff.
The most fun, curious kind
of supersoft furry pal you'll find.

He found himself upside,
reverse-side down one day
in a forest of singing sneaker trees
beside a swarm of cupcake bees.

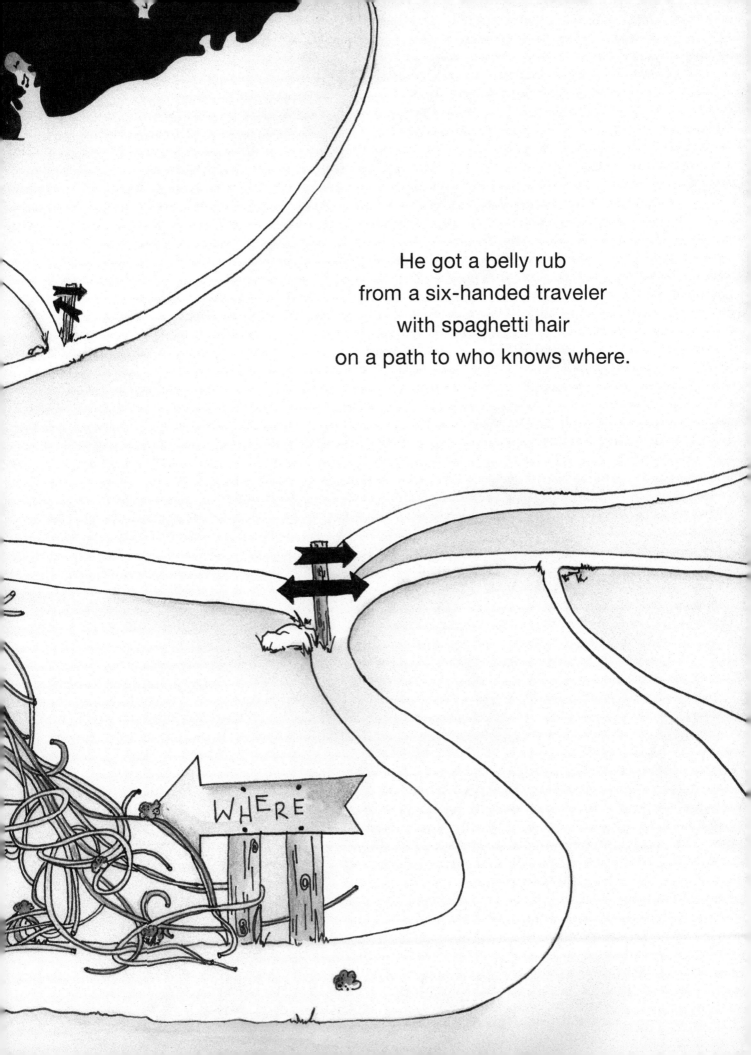

He got a belly rub
from a six-handed traveler
with spaghetti hair
on a path to who knows where.

Then he passed a sunrise,
not rising up, but from the side

and a family of giant candied cats
wearing frosting-covered donut hats.

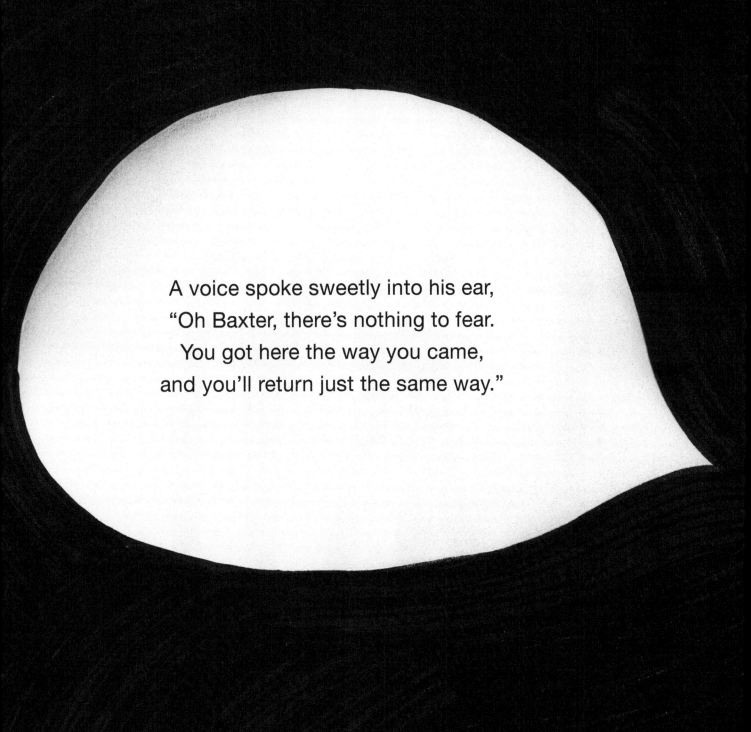

A voice spoke sweetly into his ear,
"Oh Baxter, there's nothing to fear.
You got here the way you came,
and you'll return just the same way."

Baxter barked all around.
"Who is that? Where are you?
Please!" he begged.
"I want to see this world again.
But how?
Will you tell me?
Can you tell me now?"

BARK

"Do you see me?
Do you hear me?"
The voice spoke again,
"It's no secret. I'll tell you.
Look up!"

Then a tiny seed came into view
upon an umbrella of even smaller balloons.

"You don't need a map to find your way here.
You already know where to go. You do!
Just search your mind for something new."

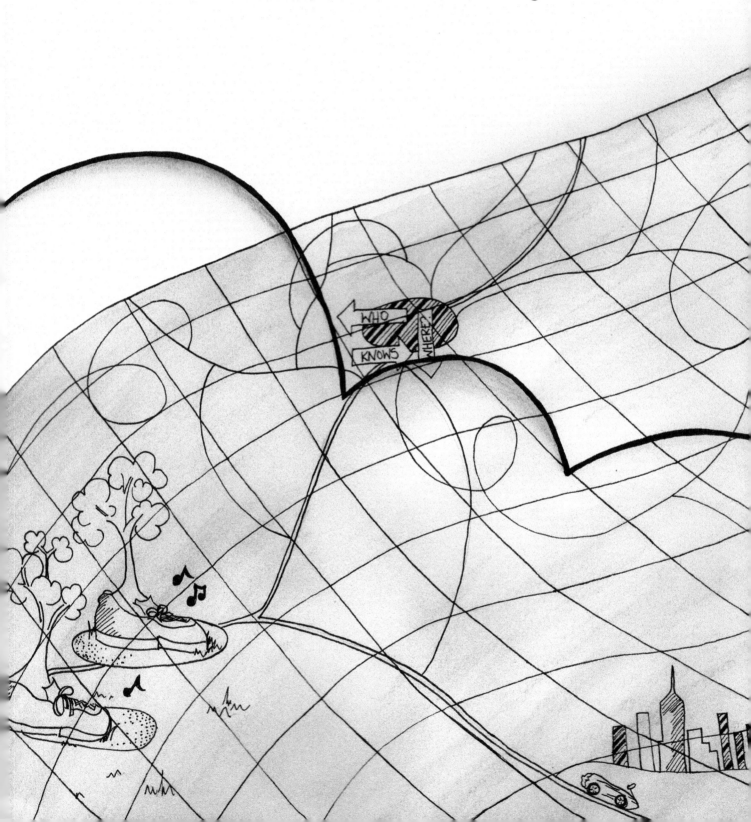

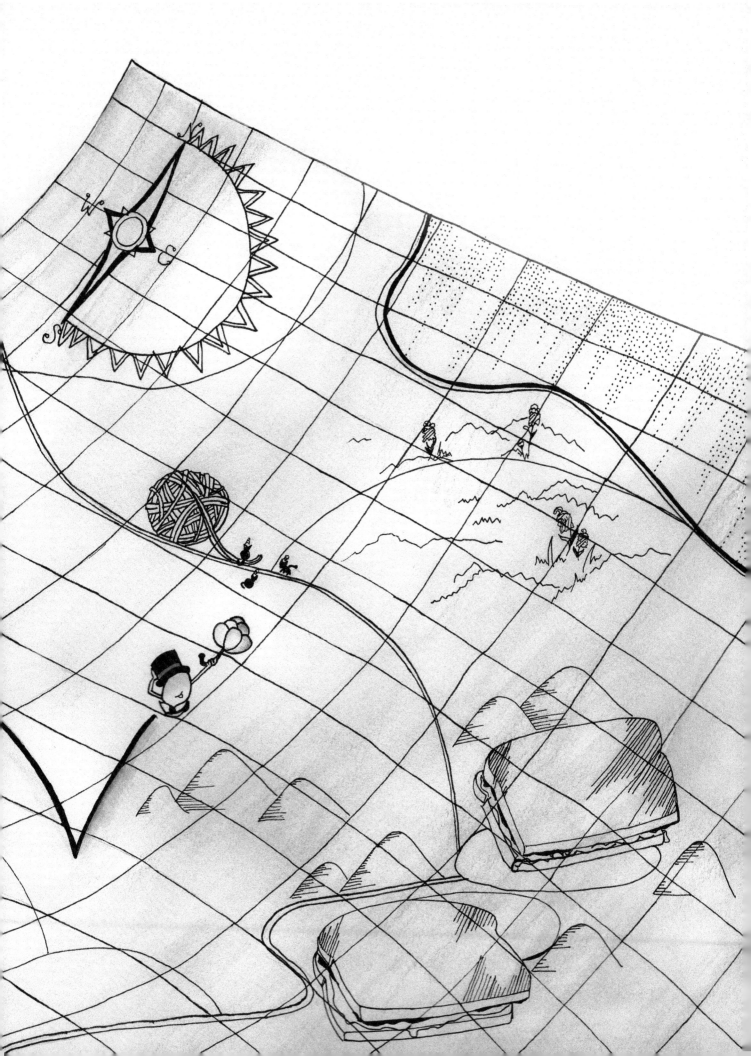

"Then you can come here when you wish
or never again if you choose.
This place, my home, lives in you.
You thought it up and colored it in too."

The balloons picked up speed
and Baxter had to run to keep up.
"I don't understand what you mean.
How could I have created what I've seen?"

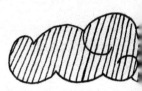

The seed laughed loudly as they passed by
a field full of cheese and cracker flower guys
waving as the breeze carried the seed by.

"Don't you see?" asked the seed,
"Listen up. Once more.
When you're eating pancakes
while standing on your head
or playing a tune on some thread..."

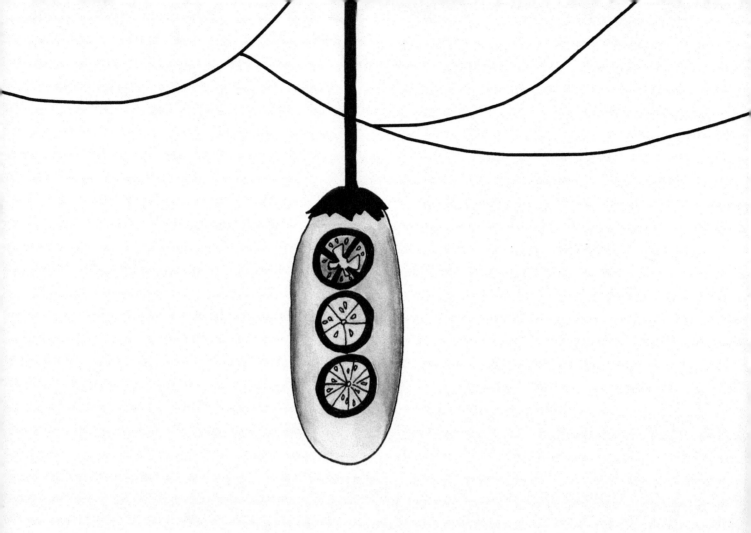

"When you dream of a polka dot elephant
driving a cucumber car,
you can find it no matter where you are."

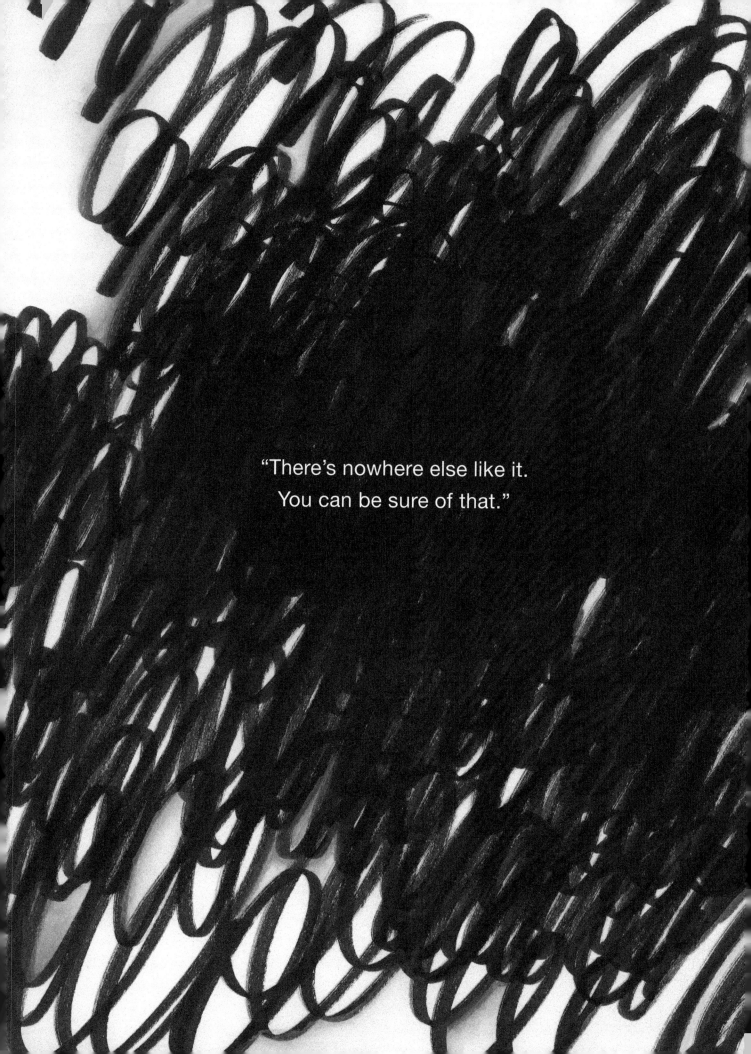

"There's nowhere else like it.
You can be sure of that."

"But, it's here whenever you want to be.
A world you made that only you can see."

"From the birds that dig instead of fly,
up to the very tippy top

of the peanut butter and jelly peaks,
to the squeaker toys playing hide and seek."

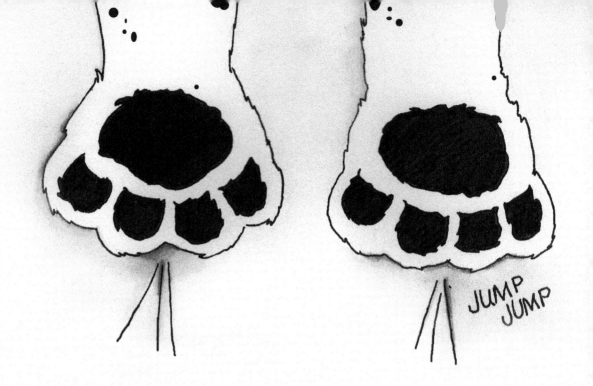

"You're in Imagination Land, you silly pup."

"I get it now! I know what to do!"
Baxter wagged his tail and jumped with joy,
"It's easy! I can come back any time.
All I have to do is close my eyes!"

He smiled at the seed.
"Thank you, friend. I'll see you soon.
Before I go, if you wouldn't mind,
could we go for a teeny-tiny balloon ride?"

Then off they flew up, Up, UP so high
toward a swiss cheese moon
hung in a grape soda sky.

CPSIA information can be obtained
at www.ICGtesting.com
Printed in the USA
LVOW06s0343250417
532093LV00004B/6/P

9 781532 337482